THE CHRISTMASAURUS

TOM FLETCHER

Illustrated by SHANE DEVRIES

PUFFIN

For Buzz, Buddy and Max – T.F.

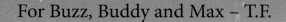

PUFFIN BOOKS

UK | USA | Canada | Ireland | Australia | India | New Zealand | South Africa

Puffin Books is part of the Penguin Random House group of companies whose addresses can be found at global.penguinrandomhouse.com.

www.penguin.co.uk   www.puffin.co.uk   www.ladybird.co.uk

Penguin
Random House
UK

First published 2021
This edition published 2022
001

Copyright © Tom Fletcher, 2021
Illustrated by Shane DeVries
The moral right of the author and illustrator has been asserted

Inspired by *The Christmasaurus* novel, written by Tom Fletcher and illustrated by Shane DeVries, published in Great Britain by Puffin Books

Printed in China

The authorized representative in the EEA is Penguin Random House Ireland, Morrison Chambers, 32 Nassau Street, Dublin D02 YH68

A CIP catalogue record for this book is available from the British Library

ISBN: 978–0–241–46656–8

All correspondence to:
Puffin Books, Penguin Random House Children's
One Embassy Gardens, 8 Viaduct Gardens, London SW11 7BW

Santa and his reindeer live as north as you can go,
in a place that's full of magic (and quite a lot of snow!).

But Santa and his reindeer do not live there on their own,
for there's a special dinosaur that also calls it home . . .

He is the Christmasaurus
and he's one of a kind!
No matter where you look,
he'll be the only one you'll find.

The Christmasaurus had a wish that someday he might fly
and pull the sleigh on Christmas Eve across the winter sky.

"I'll train you!" Santa bellowed.
"I can show you how it's done –
and now that I'm your teacher
let's begin with lesson one . . ."

"First, you need to gobble up this flying-reindeer food!
It's sure to help a dino reach a higher altitude!"

The Christmasaurus munched,

then jumped towards the Northern Lights . . .

. . . but in a flash of blue he CRASHED head-first into the ice.

Santa scratched his fluffy beard. "Well, that's a shame," he said.
"I need to leave – it's Christmas Eve and children are in bed!"

"But not to worry." Santa smiled.
"No need to look so blue . . .

We'll try again next Christmas
when I'll teach you lesson two!"

Spring turned into summer,   and autumn whizzed right by,

then it was Christmas once again and time to try to fly!

"You need to think a happy thought, like Christmas fairies do.
If happy thoughts can work for them, I bet they'll work for you!"

So Christmasaurus thought of fluffy clouds upon his scales . . .

. . . but happy thoughts don't always end
like Christmas fairy tales!

"Ho-ho-NO! That didn't work,"
said Santa with a sigh.
"And I'm afraid it's Christmas Eve
so time for me to fly!"

And with the sleigh packed full of toys
to leave beneath the tree,
he said: "We'll try next Christmas
when it's time for lesson three . . ."

Flowers bloomed and sunshine beamed,
and leaves turned brown and fell,

then smells of Christmas filled the air
to sounds of jingle bells.

"We've made you wings!" sang Santa. "They are sure to help you fly.
Just flap them like a bird and you will soar across the sky!"

And so he roared a little cry
and shed a frozen tear.

He'd have to wait for lesson four
and try again next year!

The Christmasaurus closed his eyes
and flapped with all his might . . .

But as the elves were loading all the toys upon the sleigh,
an idea popped in Santa's brain that wouldn't go away.

. . . but even Santa's gift of wings
could not make him take flight!

"Christmasaurus, why not come along with us tonight?

While I deliver presents,
you can feel the thrill of flight!"

Without a second thought, the Christmasaurus climbed aboard –
and, with their dino passenger, into the sky they soared!

Flying in the sleigh was even better than he'd dreamt,

and house by house he watched
as
down
the
chimneys
Santa
went.

"Stay in the sleigh," warned Santa. "Now you mustn't go exploring – wait here while I leave presents for the children inside snoring."

Christmasaurus didn't listen,
Christmasaurus didn't stay.

He fell into a chimney . . .

...and then Santa FLEW AWAY!

His Ho
ho
ho got quieter
the higher that they climbed,
not realizing that Christmasaurus
had been left behind!

Inside the house was quiet, but not everyone was sleeping –
for through the twinkling fairy lights
a little boy was peeping.

He saw the most amazing sight a child could dream to see:
a living, breathing DINOSAUR next to the Christmas tree!

He watched the Christmasaurus staring sadly at the sky
and understood this dinosaur was wishing it could fly!

"Hello, are you lost?" he asked the prehistoric creature.
"If you want to fly, then maybe I could be your teacher . . ."

"You don't need magic food or wings or even happy thoughts.
In fact, I'm not sure flying is a thing that can be taught.

Santa's reindeer only fly if kids like me believe.
So, if your dream is flying . . .
maybe *I'm* the thing you need!"

Midnight came, and Christmas Eve
turned into Christmas Day.
The boy made reins from fairy lights –
his wheelchair was the sleigh.

He started to believe perhaps this dinosaur *could* fly . . .

into the sky!

and, just like that, the two of them took off

They flew back over rooftops and the sleepy streets below . . .

. . . to the place that's full of magic
(and quite a lot of snow!).

They laughed and sang for hours in the North Pole's glistening glow –
but morning was approaching, when the boy would need to go.

Then Santa said, "The magic doesn't end on Christmas Day!
For someone who believes, we're always just a wish away."

They climbed aboard the sleigh and all the reindeer took their places.
The elves waved them goodbye with looks of joy upon their faces.

And with a smile, the roaring Christmasaurus led the way.
The boy had made his wish come true of pulling Santa's sleigh!

And so the Christmasaurus and his brand-new human friend
shared a magic Christmas that they wished would never end.

But the *best* thing about Christmas is,
as each one fades away . . .

you're always getting closer to another Christmas Day.